Mermaids
TO THE RESCUE

Cali Plays Fair

BY LISA ANN SCOTT

Mermaids
TO THE RESCUE

The Wish Fairy

ENCHANTED PONY ACADEMY

Mermaids
TO THE RESCUE

Cali Plays Fair

Lisa Ann Scott

illustrated by
Heather Burns

SCHOLASTIC INC.

Text copyright © 2019 by Lisa Ann Scott
Illustrations by Heather Burns, © 2019 Scholastic Inc.

ISBN 978-1-338-26703-7

10 9 8 7 6 5 4 3 2 1   19 20 21 22 23

Printed in the U.S.A.   40

First printing 2019

Book design by Yaffa Jaskoll

To my nephews, Luke and Anthony,
my very favorite twins (who might
know a thing or two about competing!)

Chapter 1

Professor Korla passed back the exams to the royal mermaids and magical seaponies at the Rescue Crew School. Her long, lovely tail swooped along the floor as she returned to her desk.

"Some of you did quite well on this quiz," she said to the class. "Others should have studied sea plant identification a bit more."

Princess Cali looked at her test and then peeked at her twin brother Cruise's paper.

They had both gotten a ninety-seven. She frowned and raised her hand. "Can we do anything for extra credit?"

"Certainly." The teacher paused. "But you performed very well, Cali."

And so did Cruise.

"I want a perfect score," Cali said. One that would make her stand apart from her brother. They'd always been "Cali and Cruise." Or "Cruise and Cali," or "the Twins." For the last nine years, everyone had treated them as one.

Now that they were in Rescue Crew School, Cali was ready to shine on her own. She had to. Cali would be performing rescues with her seapony partner, Rio. Cruise wouldn't always be with her. Cali had to prove she could do things herself—and do them well. She wanted to be the best—or at least better than her brother.

The teacher crossed her arms. "Very well. Anyone who wants extra credit can collect samples of five plants and present them in class tomorrow."

"What if I bring in six instead of five?" Cruise asked.

"You're not going to get a grade higher than one hundred, but if you want to collect six samples, feel free to do so," the teacher said.

Then I'm going to get seven, Cali thought. She could not let Cruise beat her—at anything.

She turned to her magical seapony partner, Rio. "We'll start looking right after class."

Rio gave her a funny look. "I'm happy with my ninety-three. If we go looking for plants, we won't have as much time to read the pet book. You still have to decide what kind of pet you should get. You don't really need the extra credit."

Cali frowned. Rio was an amazing seapony partner, always kind and fun. Cali

hated bickering with Rio, but the truth was, they didn't always agree.

"We can talk about pets while we look," Cali said. "I wish Cruise and I could each get our own pet. But Mom and Dad said we have to agree on one and share it."

Cruise smiled at her. "An electric eel would be amazing. We'd have so much fun with it."

Cali sighed. "What about a puffer fish? They're so cute!"

"Boring!" Cruise said. "We've got to choose something cool!"

"I'm not sure you two are ever going to agree on which pet to get," said Cruise's seapony, Jetty.

"We have to pick one before we go home at

the end of the weekend, or we don't get one at all," Cali reminded him. But she worried that Jetty was right. Lately, she and Cruise seemed to argue and disagree more and more—about everything! How could they ever agree on something as important as a pet?

The bell rang and Professor Korla closed the textbook on her desk. "Class is dismissed. And make sure to be here on time tomorrow! There will be a very exciting announcement."

The class chattered, wondering what the news might be, as they swam out of the classroom.

Cali zoomed outside and did a somersault.

Cruise swam up beside her and did two.

Cali put her hands on her hips. "I can do

better than that." She tumbled in a circle three times.

Then Cruise did four. Cali did five. Cruise did six.

Rio sighed.

Jetty shook his head. "Don't make me hit you with a stun bubble."

Cali laughed. That would be funny to see, especially since Cruise was so proud of Jetty's Sea Savvy. Stun bubbles were cool, but Rio could blow protection bubbles. After they'd chosen their seapony partners in the match ceremony, Cali and Cruise had spent hours arguing over whose Sea Savvy was better.

Cali's friends from class swam up to her.

"Come on, Cali. Let's look for plants!" Princess Nixie said.

Cali felt dizzy. "Hang on. I have to do seven somersaults."

Princess Lana grabbed her hand. "No you don't. You can't even swim straight right now!"

"I'm the somersault champ!" Cruise pumped his hands in the air. "Want to go search for plants with me?"

Cali almost said yes—then realized Cruise probably just wanted her to be there so he could gloat when he found more plants than her. "No, thanks," she said.

Cruise's smile fell. "Fine." He swam off.

"Why does Cruise copy everything I do?" Cali wondered aloud. He was making it very difficult for her to stand out.

"Well, you've always done everything together," Rio said.

Cali crossed her arms. "We're not little kids anymore."

"Just forget about it. Let's go to the park," Rio said. "You can get samples from the seaweed garden and then we can read the pet book."

They swam to the park and saw Cruise with his friends Dorado and Drake.

Cruise waved a handful of plants. "I've already got five!"

"Good for you." Cali tried her best to ignore him.

"I wonder what Professor Korla is going to announce tomorrow," Lana said.

"No more homework for the rest of the year?" Nixie joked.

"Sign me up!" Cali said.

Cali and her friends laughed.

"Watch how long I can stand on my hands!" Cruise flipped upside down and put his hands on the sandy sea floor. "Bet you can't do it longer than me, Cali."

"Don't do it, Cali," Rio whispered.

But Cali couldn't help it. She was great at standing on her hands, and her brother knew it. She swam up next to him and flipped upside down. "I can do this all day."

"I could be here all week if I wanted to," Cruise said.

"I could live the rest of my life like this," Cali said.

"Cali, let's collect our plants!" Lana said.

Cali turned her head to see Lana—and tumbled out of her handstand.

"Ha! Beat you!" Cruise said.

"Well, I'm faster than you." She zipped across the park, and he zoomed after her, right on her tail.

She was way ahead of him when Nixie's older sister, Princess Cascadia, swam into the park. She was on the Rescue Crew, too, but she'd graduated from their school the year before. "Hey, guys!" she called.

Cali and Cruise stopped their race.

Cascadia's eyes were wide. "I need everyone's help!"

Chapter 2

"**W**hat's going on?" Cali swam over to Cascadia. The other merkids and seaponies followed.

"I just got a call on my rescue shell to help a bunch of baby octopuses trying to get home," Cascadia said. "Did you guys hear it?"

"No." Cali hoped it wasn't because everyone had been distracted by her competitions with Cruise.

"It probably came through on my rescue shell because I was closer." Cascadia put her hands on her hips. "All right, everyone, come with me. It'll be a good experience. And I need help! Tiny octopuses slip right through your fingers. Put on your Say Shells so we can understand them."

The Royal Mermaid Rescue Crew helped all creatures of the sea, not just merfolk. Cali was excited to go on a mission. She hoped she could do something today to really make her mark as a Rescue Crew princess.

"Follow me!" Cascadia swam off.

Cruise pumped his arm over his head. "The Royal Mermaid Rescue Crew is on the way!"

They all followed Cascadia over to the coral reef on the edge of the city, where the tiny creatures were bobbing in the current.

"They're adorable!" Cali said.

The baby octopuses had big eyes and tiny, wiggling legs. Cali counted at least two dozen of them, but they were so quick, it was hard to keep track.

"We got washed away from our tide pool," one of the little guys squeaked.

"We don't know how to get back," said another.

"I can help," Cali said eagerly.

Nixie gave her a funny look. "We'll *all* help!"

"Let's gather them up and take them back to the tide pool," Cascadia said. "And watch out—they're little thieves with all those tentacles. They'll snatch your jewelry or hair ties and you won't even know it. They love trinkets."

The merkids tried to start collecting the creatures, but the octopuses seemed to think it was a game and scooted away, shooting ink and giggling.

Cali had one in her hand, but it tickled her so much, she lost her grip. "Stop it! We're trying to help you."

Lana had one cupped in both hands, but somehow, it slipped out! "Hey! It took my ring!" She chased after it.

Three of them shot ink in Cruise's face, and Cali couldn't help but laugh.

"How are we ever going to get them all?" Nixie asked.

"Jetty could freeze them with his stun bubbles," Cruise offered. "It doesn't hurt. It'll just keep them still for a few minutes."

Jetty blew a few bubbles, but the octopuses darted around them easily.

Cali got a great idea. "I know—Rio can handle this! Get them all in one spot." She looked at Rio and nodded. Everyone would be so impressed!

They managed to gather the octopuses near a large piece of coral, and Rio blew a big protection bubble around them.

"I usually do this to keep things away from me and Cali," Rio explained.

"But this will keep them from getting out!" Cali said, finishing Rio's thought.

"Great thinking!" Cascadia said. "Let's get this bubble to the tide pool. Way to use your Sea Savvy, Rio! That was awesome."

Cali wanted to point out that she had come up with the idea, but she kept quiet.

The merkids took turns rolling the bubble toward the tide pool. The octopuses inside seemed to be having a great time turning and tumbling.

Once the bubble reached the tide pool, Rio popped it. The octopuses spilled out, giggling and cheering. They swam off into crooks and crevices.

An octopus would be a great pet—if they

didn't shoot ink, Cali thought. Her parents would not appreciate that.

Cali counted the wiggly creatures. She only saw twenty-three. "Weren't there twenty-four of them?"

"I don't know. They were all moving too fast to count." Lana sighed.

"Good work, everyone!" Cascadia said. "Thanks for your help."

Cali's shoulders slumped, disappointed that Cascadia hadn't praised her for coming up with the plan.

"I'm headed home, and you all should get back to the dorms." Cascadia swam off.

"Yes! It's time for dinner!" Dorado said.

"I'm hungry after all that work," Nixie agreed.

"What a fun mission!" Lana said.

None of her classmates said anything about how she saved the day with her idea, either. Cali swam toward school not feeling hungry at all.

The merkids and seaponies went back to the cafeteria and filled their trays.

"Yum, sea urchins! I'm going to eat a whole plateful," Cruise announced. He turned to Cali. "Remember when we ate a pile of them at Dad's birthday party? Bet I can still eat more than you."

Cali thought sea urchins were too salty, but she started piling them onto her plate anyway. "No way—I can eat more."

"You don't even like those," Rio reminded her.

"My tastes may have changed." Cali added some kelp and fish eggs to her plate.

Cali sat with her friends at the table next to Cruise. He popped a sea urchin into his mouth. And then another, and another.

Cali pressed her lips together, then put an urchin in her mouth and chewed it as quickly as she could. She made a face and pushed away her plate. She'd let Cruise win this one.

He pumped his hands in the air. "I'm the urchin-eating champion of the world!"

"Oh boy, what an honor," joked Lana's seapony partner, Marina.

Cruise bowed in his seat. "Thank you, thank you."

Cali glared at him.

"Hey, Cali!" Nixie said, distracting her. "What do you think the professor's big announcement is going to be tomorrow?"

Cali cheered up. "I don't know, but I'm excited!"

"I can't wait to find out," Lana said.

Whatever it was, Cali hoped it gave her a chance to be the best—at something. At the very least, better than Cruise.

Chapter 3

The next day in class, Cali hurried to her seat, waiting for the announcement. When Principal Vanora swam into the room with Professor Korla, Cali knew it was going to be something big.

All the students quieted down.

"Class, as you know, the school year is ending soon. And we want to do something special," Professor Korla said. "Something fun!"

"So we're having a Rescue Crew tournament to name the top merstudent of the year," the principal said. "First-year and second-year students can participate."

Cheers and applause filled the room. Cali squirmed with excitement. This was the perfect way to prove herself. She just had to win!

"This competition is designed to help the city of Astoria, too," the principal continued. "Some of the events will provide Astoria with needed services and supplies."

"You can win points with each competition," Professor Korla said. "And whoever has the most points at the end is named Student of the Year." She paused and held up a medal. "That student will be rewarded with this."

Cali and Rio shared an excited look. She noticed Cruise high-fiving Dorado, like he'd already won.

"What are the competitions?" Cali asked.

"Contest one is pearl harvesting—a test of who can gather the most," the principal said.

"That'll be so fun!" Lana said.

"We'll use the pearls to patch up the gates to Astoria," the principal explained.

Cali was excited about that challenge. Oysters opened when you sang to them. This would also be a great chance to show off her singing skills.

"Contest two," said Principal Vanora, "is painting shells to scatter about the kingdom. The winners will be whoever paints the most and who paints the prettiest shell."

"And contest three—who can collect the most ocean litter?" Professor Korla smiled. "We'll all help to clean up our beautiful Astoria."

That didn't sound as fun as shell painting and pearl harvesting, but Cali knew she could do it.

"Those are the challenges next Saturday," the principal said. "On Sunday, we're collecting glow coral for our street lamps and you'll race through an obstacle course. And then we'll declare a winner."

The class chattered and cheered.

"These challenges are for royal mermaids only," the principal said. "Your seaponies can support you and cheer you on, but they can't do the tasks for you."

"And there's a bonus fifty points if you find the missing Night Star or the Trident of Protection." Professor Korla held up an old painting showing the Trident and all its gems.

"As you know," the principal said, "the Fathom Pearl and Sea Diamond have been found. If we can find the Night Star and Trident, we may be able to restore the protective powers they once brought to our seas."

Nixie's friends found the Sea Diamond near the rift. And Lana brought back the Fathom Pearl from the Northern Seas.

Cali imagined how proud she'd feel presenting the Trident or the Night Star to the principal. That would certainly prove her worth. But where could they be? They might be lost forever. Or worse—they could be lost in the rift, the most dangerous part of the ocean.

"The competition begins next weekend," Principal Vanora said. "It should be a wonderful event."

"Now it's time for our studies," their teacher said. "Those of you who want to present your plant samples for extra credit may do so now."

Cruise showed off his eight plants—one

more than Cali had collected. But the teacher raised both their grades to one hundred.

For the rest of the day, Cali couldn't stop thinking about the tournament. It would be so exciting to be named Student of the Year. That was one thing she and Cruise couldn't share, since only one merkid could win it. She wished she didn't have to go home for the week. She wanted to start the tournament now!

At the end of the day, the students gathered up their things to return to their kingdoms.

Cali swam up to Cruise. "Remember, we have to tell Mom and Dad which pet we want when we get home, or we don't get any pet at all!" she reminded her twin.

Unfortunately, they had to decide on one together. It would be "Cali and Cruise's" pet. The Twins' pet.

"We *could* do that." Cruise raised an eyebrow. "Or we could have a contest! Winner gets to choose."

Cali was intrigued. "What kind of contest?"

Cruise thought for a moment, then snapped his fingers. "Whoever makes it home first gets to pick."

Jetty and Rio shared a worried look.

"Okay—let's do it!" Cali knew she could beat him.

"Contest starts . . . now!" Cruise shot through the water, and Cali was hot on his tail.

Chapter 4

The swim home to Coquina took a few hours. Cali zoomed ahead of Cruise, but then he caught up. They swapped the lead, back and forth, over and over.

Finally, they could see their castle, just ahead.

"Guys, take a break!" Rio shouted.

But Cali *had* to win. Who knew what Cruise might think was a good pet? She swam as fast as she could—and then, in a fresh burst of speed, Cruise beat her by only a few inches.

"Yes!" He spun in a circle. "I win! I get to choose the pet!"

Cali sighed. "Please don't pick something horrible."

"Of course not." Cruise waggled his eyebrows. "I'm going to pick something cool."

Their mother and father, the king and queen of Coquina, swam out of the castle, calling, "Welcome home!" Their mom hugged them, and their father gave them each a kiss on the cheek.

"Guess what? There's going to be a big tournament at the academy next week," Cali told them.

"Whoever wins gets a medal and is named Student of the Year," Cruise added, still breathless from their race.

"Wow!" their mom said. "How exciting."

"Can't wait to hear how that goes," their dad added. "In the meantime, have you decided which pet you'd like yet?"

"I still think we should be able to each get our own pet," Cali said.

"No, this is a decision for you two to make," their father reminded them.

Cruise grinned. "We'll have our answer tomorrow."

Their mother let out a long breath. "I'm so glad to hear you're able to work this out together."

Cali sighed. *Together.* Why couldn't her parents understand she wanted to do some things on her own?

"Yes, that's wonderful!" their father agreed. "I knew you could find a solution."

Rio and Jetty shared a worried look.

The rest of the night, Cruise leafed through a book of sea creatures.

"What about a goblin shark? Look!" He held up a book with a picture of the creepy creature.

"No! That would be a horrible pet."

"Come on, just read about it," he said. "We'd be the only kids around who had one."

"I'm sure there's a reason other merkids don't have them," Cali said.

"Okay, then how about this?" He held up a

picture of something so terrifying, she didn't even know what it was.

Cali turned away and wouldn't even look at him. Why did she have to be a twin?

The next morning the family sat down for breakfast before the twins had to leave for their classes at Coquina Primary School.

"So what did you two decide on?" their father asked.

Cruise smiled wide. "It took a long time to pick the best pet, but we want—a moray eel!"

Cali almost gasped, but just in time she forced herself to smile.

Her mother looked at her, shocked. "Really?"

Cali could only nod.

"We thought it would be an interesting pet," Cruise said.

"Very well," their father said. "We'll choose one from the shelter today when you get home."

Cali wouldn't talk to Cruise on the way to school.

"Hey, you agreed to the race," Cruise reminded her.

She balled up her fists. "You picked something horrible just to make me mad."

Cruise looked surprised. "I did not. I really think it'll be cool! Just give it a chance."

Cali sighed. "Fine." But she doubted she would ever like having an eel for a pet.

They swam to their classrooms. Today, she was glad they had different teachers at their Coquina school.

"How was rescue school?" her friend Kai asked as Cali took her seat.

"It was good. But there's this big competition coming up next weekend." Cali told her friends all about it.

"I hope you win!" her friend Raina said.

"Me too. I want everyone to know me for something other than being Cruise's twin. And if he wins, I'll never hear the end of it."

It was nice to have a break from Cruise for the day. But as soon as classes ended, her brother swam up to Cali.

"Let's go get our pet!" He nudged her with his elbow. "I'll let you name it."

Cali forced a smile. Maybe a moray eel wouldn't be the worst pet in the world. Anything was possible.

Their parents took them to the rescue shelter in town. Cali was excited to see so many interesting animals up for adoption, like sea dragons. But she looked anxiously at the tanks, crossing her fingers. *Please don't have any moray eels, please don't have any moray eels.*

"Cali, come look at this guy!" Cruise shouted.

She swam to the tank that held a small moray eel. It looked at her and hissed. She tried not to cry. "Cool," she mumbled.

"This is the one I want!" Cruise said.

"You mean the one you both want?" their mother asked.

"Yes, that's what I meant," Cruise said. "What should we name it, Cali?"

"I don't know." The eel snapped at Cali, and she jumped back. "Bitey?"

Cruise pumped an arm in the air. "Yes! Come on, Bitey. You're going to love living with us."

Cruise spent the rest of the night playing with Bitey while Cali read a book.

"Don't you want to play with him?" Cali's mom asked.

"No, thanks." Bitey scared her, but she wouldn't admit it to anyone—especially Cruise. She avoided Bitey as much as she could for the rest of the week. And her brother, too.

Saturday morning, the twins ate breakfast and got ready to head back to the Rescue Academy.

Cruise picked up Bitey to put in his bag.

"You're bringing him with us?" Cali asked.

"I can't leave him home," Cruise said. "He's our pet."

"You're in charge of him," Cali said.

"I can't wait to show him to everyone!"

"Make sure you leave him in your room during the competition this weekend," Cali told him.

"Of course!" Cruise said.

Their mother and father swam outside with them. "Do your best during the tournament!" their father said. "And have fun!"

Cali glared at Cruise and the eel. She was more determined than ever to be the best. After all, look what happened when she let Cruise win!

Chapter 5

Back at the academy dorms, Cruise showed off Bitey to their friends.

"You picked a moray eel for a pet?" Lana asked Cali.

"Cruise picked it," Cali said.

"Isn't he cool?" Cruise asked. "He's like a cuddly little monster!"

"I guess so." Dorado backed away from the hissing creature.

"Come on, let's get to school so we can start the competition!" Nixie said.

Cruise put Bitey away, and they swam to school.

The Rescue Crew teachers and principal were waiting outside. "Come along to our first challenge!" They led the students to the oyster beds. "We need new pearls to repair the gates to Astoria. Grab a bag and start collecting! You have one hour," the principal said. "Let the tournament begin!"

Cali got right to work, singing to the oysters and tapping their shells. Slowly, they opened up so she could take the pearls inside. She grinned, knowing how much Cruise hated singing—the only thing that made the oysters open.

The other students zipped around the oyster beds, gathering pearls. Their voices filled the water. Cali sang louder, hoping the other merkids would notice how well she sang.

Suddenly, she heard Cruise shouting, "Open, oyster, open!" All the oysters around him started snapping their shells open and shut, agitated. Some even tried to burrow into the sand. They were clearly annoyed, but Cruise was able to easily snatch up dozens of pearls.

"Hey, you're supposed to *sing* to them," Cali said.

He shrugged. "My way seems to be working fine. Try it!"

"No!" Cali kept working, singing louder and faster, plucking out pearl after pearl. But she couldn't help noticing how full Cruise's bag was. She sang even faster and tapped the shells more quickly, but she couldn't collect as many as Cruise had.

And no one had said a word about her singing voice.

The principal blew a whistle and said, "Time's up! Bring over your pearls."

Cali carried her bag over and checked out everyone else's haul. Cruise's was overflowing with pearls.

"We'll count these up," the principal said, "but I can tell already that Cruise collected the most—and devised a new way to harvest pearls. Well done!"

Cali gritted her teeth. No one noticed her sweet singing, and now Cruise was getting praise for shouting?

"Cruise earns ten points toward the tournament," Professor Korla announced.

"Yes!" Cruise twirled in a happy circle.

Cali flashed him a mean look. It didn't seem fair that he'd gotten the pearls by shouting instead of singing. That wasn't how it worked!

"It's okay," Rio said quietly. "I know you're upset. But this is just the first event."

Cali nodded and took a deep breath. "You're right." She was going to have to try even harder on the next challenge.

They went to the park and took a break for lunch. Cali was quiet as she munched a kelp sandwich. Cruise sat nearby popping urchins into his mouth. "*Six* urchins! I broke my own record! Wanna try and beat me, Cali?"

Ugh, why was he always taunting her? Cali turned her back, ignoring him for the rest of the meal.

"Students," the principal announced, "it's

time for our next event of the day. We'll stay right here in the park and paint seashells to scatter around Astoria." She stood beside a table filled with seashells, paints, and paintbrushes.

"Yes!" Cali loved painting. She *had* to win this one.

"Points will be awarded for number of shells painted and the best shell, as judged by the teachers," Professor Korla explained.

Cali grabbed a pile of shells and got to work. She sketched out an image of dolphins jumping up out of the water, then carefully painted it.

"You're spending a lot of time on just one shell," Rio said.

"I figured I could either go for the most shells, or the prettiest. I have a good shot at the prettiest."

After a few minutes she looked over and saw that Cruise had painted a whole pile of shells. They had simple designs, nothing like her elaborate scene.

"Hey, you barely painted those," Cali said.

Cruise didn't look up from his work. "I know that I can't paint the best shell, but I can paint the most. No one said they had to look great."

Cali panicked, wondering if she should have done the same thing. Especially since

Nixie had painted a gorgeous scene on each of hers. Maybe Cali's wouldn't be the prettiest after all.

With shaky hands, she added a few details to hers before the teachers blew the whistle to end the event.

Cali swam back and forth while the teachers tallied the results. "I don't think I'm going to win this one, either."

"That's okay," Rio said. "You can't win them all."

"But I have to win at least one of them!" Cali said.

"Don't be so hard on yourself. It's more important to try your best."

"We have the results of the shell painting

contest," Professor Korla said, calling the students to attention.

"Cruise painted the most shells," the principal said, "earning ten points. And Nixie painted the most beautiful shell. Ten points for her as well."

Cali took a few deep breaths so she wouldn't cry. How had this happened? Cruise had won two events and she'd won none.

"Class, we're going to scatter the shells around the city. Grab a few, then meet back here for our next competition," the principal said.

The merstudents started gathering the shells. "Hey, a few of mine are missing," Nixie said.

"How strange!" her seapony, Rip, said.

Cruise swam up to Cali. "Come on, let's see which one of us can scatter the most! It'll be fun."

"No, thanks." Cali gathered a handful of shells. She didn't want him to know how upset she was. And she didn't want him to beat her at yet another thing.

Cruise shrugged and swam away.

Cali just couldn't let her brother win the whole tournament. She was ready to do anything to beat him.

Chapter 6

After they were done scattering the shells, everyone swam back to the park.

"Our final event of the day is litter collection," said Professor Korla.

There were a few groans.

"This is going to help Astoria," the principal reminded the class. "You have two hours. We'll sound the conch shell when time is up. You can travel anywhere in the city to gather trash."

"Take a few bags! We're hoping you'll get a lot," Professor Korla said.

Hopeful, Cali grabbed five bags.

Her friends were gathering together in a group.

"Come with us!" Nixie told her. "We're starting in the park."

But Cali didn't want to be distracted. "Sorry, guys. I think I'll collect more if I'm working alone."

"Okay! We'll see you later!" Her friends swam off.

Cruise swam up to her. "Want to work together?"

"No!" Cali said.

"What's wrong?" Cruise said as Cali sped off.

"Wait up!" Rio called after her.

Cali and Rio swam to the outskirts of the city. Out there, lots of debris had floated down from the surface. It didn't take long to fill one bag. And then another, and another. Cali was starting to feel good about her chances with this event.

"Let's head back toward the center of the city," Cali told Rio.

They swam past a few houses. Most people lived right in the middle of the city. But some people liked being farther from town. Cali waved to an older mermaid who was swimming out of her house with a bag. She set it next to her mailbox.

The lady smiled at Cali. "Are you the new trash collector?"

Cali laughed. "No, I'm just collecting litter for a contest at school."

The lady pointed to the bag. "Add that one to your collection. Thanks, dear!" She swam back into her house before Cali could tell her the contest didn't work that way.

"Too bad you can't use that," Rio said. "You'd have four full bags!"

Cali paused. "Well, the principal did say we could gather it from anywhere in the city. And this is the city."

"I don't think that's what she meant."

"But it's not breaking the rules." Cali bent down and picked up the bag. Some of the trash fell out and she put it back in. "See? I just collected some of that trash."

"Do you really think that's fair? You weren't too happy when Cruise was shouting at the oysters."

"I didn't do anything wrong. The mermaid told me to take the bag. And maybe the currents would have scattered all her trash if I hadn't taken it."

"I still don't think it should count."

Cali was not in the mood to bicker with

Rio. "I'll think about it. But for now, I'm going to hold on to it."

Cali managed to collect another bag of litter before they heard the conch horn blow.

"We'd better get back," Rio said.

As Cali swam into the park she noticed Cruise had four bags of trash. Everyone else had two or three. With the extra bag she picked up, Cali would win. At this point, it was her only chance to stay in the competition.

Cruise saw her and waved. "I've got four! Bet you didn't get more!"

Cali gritted her teeth. "Come on, Rio. We're handing in all those bags."

"Five bags?" the principal asked. "Cali, you win this event and get ten points."

Her friends cheered. "Yay, Cali!"

Cruise crossed his arms and frowned.

"Here's a look at our final tally for the day," Professor Korla said. She held up a big sheet with everyone's points. Cruise was in the lead with twenty. Nixie and Cali each had ten.

Cali looked at Rio. "I have a chance now!"

SCOREBOARD

Nixie:	✩✩✩✩✩✩✩✩✩✩	10
Cruise:	✩✩✩✩✩✩✩✩✩✩✩✩✩✩✩✩✩✩✩✩	20
Cali:	✩✩✩✩✩✩✩✩✩✩	10

She could be the merstudent of the year. Not Cruise. Not her and Cruise. Just her. Finally, she could stand out!

Rio didn't say anything.

"What?" Cali whispered. "I didn't do anything wrong."

"Let's just go get some rest," Rio said.

Cruise caught up to Cali as they swam back to the dorms. "You may have won that event, but I'm still in the lead!"

"Yeah, for now!" Cali said.

"Want to play with Bitey?" he asked. "He's probably lonely."

"No, I don't think he likes me," Cali said. "And besides, he's really your pet."

"He's *our* pet, and he just has to get to know you. I was thinking of some fun games we can play with him together. Come on, at least say hi."

"Okay." Cali followed Cruise to his room.

Cruise went to the tank he set up for the eel. "Bitey?" He looked in his closet and under the bed. "He's not here! Bitey's gone! We have to find him!"

Chapter 7

Cali, Cruise, and their seaponies set off to search the school grounds.

"Bitey! Where are you?" Cruise called.

"He could be anywhere," Cali said. "We were out all day. He could have swum very far from here."

Cruise looked so upset, Cali forgot she didn't even like the eel. "We can get another one."

"I don't want another eel. I want Bitey!" Cruise said.

"It's getting dark soon," Cali said. "We don't have much more time to search."

"Maybe we can leave a dish of food on the windowsill in your room and see if he comes back," Jetty suggested.

Cruise sniffed. "Maybe."

Cali wanted to tell him that if they'd picked a cute sea slug for a pet, it wouldn't have gotten far if it tried to run away. But she knew that wouldn't make Cruise feel better.

"Let's look until it gets dark," Cruise said.

"We'll split up and meet back here," Cali said.

Everyone swam off, calling for Bitey. Cali wasn't even sure the eel knew its own name yet. But she lifted rocks and peeked in holes. Eels were fast swimmers *and* very good at hiding.

The twins and their seaponies met back at the dorm as the sunlight was fading. No one had good news.

"We can search again tomorrow. Before the tournament," Cali said.

She had a hard time sleeping that night. She flipped and flopped in bed. She didn't miss Bitey, but she felt bad for Cruise. As much as she wanted to be her own mermaid, Cali didn't like to see her twin so sad.

And she couldn't stop thinking about the

litter challenge. She hadn't asked for that extra bag—and she had cleaned up some of the trash that spilled out of it! So why did she feel like she wasn't playing fair?

As soon as she woke up the next morning, Cali swam to Cruise's room. "Did Bitey come back for the food?"

Cruise sped over to the window and found a jellyfish eating from the plate. "No."

They went back outside and searched for an hour, but there was still no sign of the missing moray eel.

Cruise and Cali swam to Rescue Crew School. Her brother was so sad, he didn't even try to race Cali there.

"Good morning, students!" said the principal. "It's day two of our tournament and our first event is an important one. We're collecting glow coral for our streetlights. Whoever gets the most in an hour wins ten points. And there's ten points for whoever finds the biggest piece."

Cruise was quiet as he swam away.

"Good luck!" Cali called after him. But she was still desperate to win the contest, so she saddled up Rio with two bags to hold the coral and swam off. She didn't even wait for her friends. She'd be able to work better on her own.

Cali found a few good spots with lots of glow coral. She worked so fast collecting it and found so much, she filled both bags and had an armful of it when their time was up.

"Excellent work, Cali!" the principal said.

Cruise swam up with one bags barely filled. Lots of other students had more than he did.

"What happened?" Cali asked. "You hardly have any."

"While I was collecting the coral, I was also looking for Bitey. I didn't find him."

Cali felt bad. Cruise was probably never going to find the eel.

"Lana found the biggest piece of coral and earned ten points. And Cali collected the most coral," Principal Vanora announced. "That's another ten points for you!"

"Yes!" Cali cried. "Now I'm tied for first place," she told Rio. But Rio didn't smile.

"What place would you be in if you hadn't been given that extra bag of garbage?" Rio whispered.

"Come on, Rio! You're supposed to be my friend."

"I am. And friends tell friends when they don't do the right thing."

Cali shook her head. "Let's go. It's time for the obstacle course!"

The teachers timed the students as they raced through the course one at a time. Each merkid had to swim over and under nets, untie a conch shell from a string using one hand, and make their way through a maze

of lava tubes. It was so much fun, Cali forgot about all her other worries for a while.

Nixie came in first place. Cali was a little disappointed, but Cruise didn't even seem upset. Obviously, he was still sad about Bitey.

The principal scratched her head. "I can't

believe it, but at the end of our tournament, we have a three-way tie."

The class started chattering excitedly.

"Cali, Cruise, and Nixie all have the same score," the principal said. "Twenty points. Take a break for lunch and then we'll announce a tiebreaker event."

Chapter 8

Nixie grabbed Cali's hands. "Can you believe it?"

Cali blinked a few times. "No, I can't!" Her worries were rushing back: that bag of litter, the way Cruise was so sad he wasn't even trying to win anymore. She looked over at him, but he was just staring off into the distance. Winning the competition wouldn't feel as good knowing Cruise hadn't really been trying.

She swam up to him. "Why didn't you work harder in the glow coral competition?" Cali asked him. "You've been trying to beat me at everything lately." Her anger was growing, remembering how he'd been constantly trying to show her up.

"What? I've just been trying to have fun with you," Cruise said.

"You're always taunting me!" Cali said.

Cruise looked confused. "No I'm not. We always play games—at least, we did until we came to Rescue Crew School."

"What are you talking about?" Cali asked.

"Now we hardly do anything together anymore, Cali. It's like you don't want to be around me." His voice softened. "I miss hanging out with you, I guess."

Cali's shoulders slumped. "I'm sorry. I'm just trying to make a name for myself. We've always been 'the Twins,' like we're not our own merkids." She shrugged. "I've sort of been trying to prove myself. I never wanted to make you feel that way."

"Okay, I'll stop challenging you all the time," Cruise said, looking away. "I guess we're growing up and just won't be as close anymore. I can hang out with Bitey and Jetty. I mean, if I ever *find* Bitey."

Cali's stomach fell. Was that really what she wanted? She wasn't sure. But she knew one thing for sure: They had to find Cruise's eel.

"Hey, everyone!" she called out. "Cruise's eel, Bitey, is missing."

"It's *our* eel," Cruise said quietly.

Cali nodded. "Right. I'm going to go look for him if anyone wants to join me."

Most of the students followed her, and Cali smiled, relieved. She could use a break from

worrying and competing with everyone—
even her brother.

"The seaponies can get snacks for everyone and meet up later," Jetty said.

"Thanks," Cruise said, looking surprised
and a little more cheerful than before.

"Let's split up into groups and meet back
here in an hour," Cali said. "If you find him,
let us know on our rescue shells."

"Sounds good!" said Dorado.

"I'll come with you guys," Nixie said.

"Me too," said Lana.

The rest of the merkids split up into two
groups and swam off.

"I was reading more about eels," Cruise
said. "And I learned they like to live in caves."

"Okay," Cali said. "We should go to the outskirts of the city."

"Grab some chunks of glow coral so we can see inside the caves," Cruise said.

"Great idea!" Nixie said.

They each grabbed a piece of coral from the pile everyone had collected and headed off.

"What happens if we find Kraken's Cave by mistake?" Lana wondered, sounding scared.

"That's just an old legend," Nixie said. "I'm sure if there was a Kraken around here we would have seen it. The Kraken is supposed to be huge!"

"And he has treasure in his cave," Cali

said. "So if we did find the Kraken, we'd be rich!"

Cruise chuckled. "Yeah, because I'm sure he'd just let us take all his stuff. Let's focus on my eel, guys. Don't worry about finding the Kraken. That's never going to happen. If we find him, I'll eat a bucket of shells."

Nixie giggled. "Now I hope we *do* find the Kraken."

They swam along, and Cali spotted a cave ahead. "Let's go check it out." But after all the jokes about the Kraken, she was feeling a little nervous. "You go in first," she told Cruise.

He took a deep breath, then swam into the mouth of the cave. He held up his chunk of glow coral. "Bitey?"

Cali peered in. "There are just a few little fish in here."

Rio, Jetty, and Rip swam up to them with snacks. "Our saddlebags are loaded with goodies. Grab a few things."

Cali took a kelp wrap and quickly ate it. She noticed something out of the corner of her eye. Was it a flash? Did something zoom by? Since everyone else was still eating, she grabbed her glow coral. "I'll be right back."

Cali saw the flash again and swam toward it. Whatever it was, it was coming from a cave. A big one. She looked behind her, but she couldn't see her friends anymore. *That's okay*, she thought. *I'll call for help on my rescue shell if I need it.*

Slowly, she got closer to the cave. She held
up her glow coral in the darkness. She saw
trinkets and things scattered all around.

And then she saw two huge eyes staring
at her.

Chapter 9

Cali wanted to scream. She should have grabbed her rescue shell and called for help. But she couldn't. She was frozen in fear. She tried to yell, but it came out in a whisper.

The eyes disappeared, but her glow coral lit up something shiny for a brief moment.

Cali blinked a few times. Was that the Night Star? She dropped the glow coral and grabbed her rescue shell. "Guys! I need help!"

Nixie's seapony, Rip, was there in seconds.

His Sea Savvy was swimming faster than seemed possible.

"What is it?" he asked.

"I'm not sure," Cali said. "Something . . . something is in that cave. With big eyes. And there's t-t-t-treasure, too."

"Are you sure it's not your imagination?" he asked. "We were just talking about the Kraken. You're probably just seeing things."

The other seaponies and merkids swam up to them. "What's going on?" Cruise asked. "Did you find Bitey?"

Cali shook her head. "I think you're going to be eating shells. I think it might be . . ." She lowered her voice. "The Kraken."

"That's unlikely," Rip said, sounding uncertain.

"Bitey has little beady eyes," Cali said. "I just saw a huge pair of eyes in there. And something shiny. It almost looked like . . ."

"Like what?" Nixie asked.

Cali wasn't sure she should tell them she thought she'd seen the Night Star. Because if it was in there, she wanted to get it. She wanted the fifty extra points, because then it wouldn't matter that she'd taken that bag of litter. She'd have more than enough points to win without it. And everyone would know she had found it. That was a way to make a name for herself for sure. They'd probably write about her in the history books.

"I'm sure it was nothing," she said.

"Should someone go in there?" Nixie asked.

No one said anything.

"Bitey?" Cruise called. "Are you in there, buddy?"

Something inside the cave made a noise.

"What do we do?" Nixie whispered.

"Rio, can you blow a protection bubble around all of us?" Waverly asked.

Rio shook her head. "I can't make one that big."

"Cruise, what if Jetty blew some stun bubbles in there?" Cali asked. "Even if Bitey is in there and gets hit, he'll be fine."

"Great idea!" Cruise said. "Do it, Jetty!"

Jetty shot bubbles into the cave, but they just hit the walls and the ceiling. The noises continued.

They all looked at each other nervously.

"We need to figure out exactly what's in there," Cali said. "Everyone, toss your glow coral inside so it lights up the cave."

The four of them threw their coral into the cave. They saw a pile of odd things, like jewelry, pretty shells—even some of the ones they'd just painted!

"How did all that get here?" Nixie asked.

"I don't know," Cali said slowly. Then she saw the big eyes again—on one of the tiny octopuses from the other day. She laughed. "Look!"

"And there's Bitey, too!" Cruise shouted.

Everyone cheered.

"Come here, boy," Cruise said.

Bitey hissed at him.

That's when Cali spotted it: The Night Star was at the back of the cave. She had to swim inside and get it!

But before she could, Rip gasped. "Does that look like a crack in the ceiling?" he asked.

"I wonder if the stun bubbles did that?" Cali asked.

And just then, a rock fell from the roof of the cave. And then another.

"The cave's collapsing!" Rio said.

Rip, Nixie, and Waverly swam back from the cave.

"Come on, guys!" Nixie said.

"We have to rescue the animals!" Cruise said.

"But you also have to be safe," Rip said. "It's too dangerous."

"He's my pet," Cruise said.

"And I saw the Night Star inside!" Cali said. "It's in the back of the cave." It would be gone forever if the cave collapsed.

"I can blow a protection bubble to prop up the entrance," Rio said. "Cali, stay here. The bubble is stronger when you're with me."

"I'll go in," Cruise said.

Cruise disappeared into the cave. Cali knew that if he found the Night Star, he'd get the fifty points. He'd get all the glory, not her. But that didn't matter anymore. She just wanted him to be safe.

"Be careful!" she called after him.

A few more rocks dropped around the entrance of the cave.

"Hurry!" Rio shouted. "I'm not sure how much longer my protection bubble is going to hold!"

Chapter 10

Cruise zoomed out of the cave just as Rio's bubble and the opening collapsed. He had Bitey in one hand and the octopus in the other.

"Did you get the Night Star?" Cali asked.

Cruise shook his head. "I reached for it, but I heard all those rocks coming down. I had to leave it."

Cali's heart fell. The gem was probably crushed or buried forever.

Bitey started coughing.

"Are you okay, buddy?" Cruise looked worried.

Bitey coughed a few more times and spit out a shiny gem.

Cali blinked a few times. "Bitey got the Night Star!"

"Cruise! You're going to get an extra fifty points!" Jetty said.

"Let's go show the principal!" Nixie said.

Cali thought she'd be upset, but she wasn't. In fact, she was a bit relieved she wasn't going to win the competition. Now it *really* didn't matter that she'd gotten that extra bag of trash. And surprisingly, she felt happy for Cruise.

The octopus Cruise was holding wiggled out of his grip and swam over to Cali. It blinked its big eyes. She laughed. "I can't believe I thought you were the Kraken. You're such a little thing." She held the tiny creature in her hands and smiled.

"Let's get back to school," Rip said.

Nixie picked up her rescue shell. "We found Bitey! And we found something else great, too. Meet us back at school!"

They rushed back to Rescue Crew School, where the principal and teachers were waiting outside.

"We've come up with a perfect tie-breaker," Principal Vanora said.

"You're not going to need it," Nixie said. "Look what Cruise found!"

Cruise handed the gem to the principal. "Is this the Night Star?"

Principal Vanora studied it carefully, holding it up to the light. She smiled. "I believe it is! Where did you find this?"

"We found a cave filled with things. And Bitey was there, too!" Cruise said.

"And this little octopus! She must have grabbed all the stuff," Cali said. "We rescued a group of baby octopuses last week and put them back in their tide pool. This one must have been separated from the others."

"I wonder if she found the Night Star and brought it to the cave?" Nixie asked.

"Perhaps," Professor Korla said. "But however it got there, Cruise found it. And that's an extra fifty points. It would seem that Cruise wins the tournament!"

The rest of the class cheered, and Cruise took a bow.

Cali wanted to point out that she'd actually spotted the Night Star, but she realized that Cruise had been the one brave enough to swim into the cave. He deserved all the praise. Still, she felt sad that she hadn't found a way yet to stand out.

Maybe she never would.

"Join us in the auditorium in half an hour for the medal ceremony," the principal said.

Most of the mermaids and seaponies swam off, laughing and chattering.

Cali went up to Cruise. "Congratulations. I'm so glad you found Bitey. And the Night Star."

But Cruise didn't smile.

"What's wrong?" she asked.

"Nothing," he mumbled. He looked at the octopus. "Well, I guess I should have picked a pet that was easier to care for. Like this little one." He tickled the octopus.

"Careful! She might squirt you with ink."

The octopus squeaked a few words.

"She's talking!" Rio said. "Put on your Say Shell."

Cali grabbed hers from her rescue cape. "What did you say?" she asked the octopus.

"I said that I don't have any ink. I wasn't born with any."

Cali's jaw dropped. An octopus that wouldn't be messy? "I wonder if Mom would let me keep her as a pet!"

"I'd love to be your pet!" the octopus said.

"But we already have Bitey," Cruise said.

"Maybe if we talk to Mom and Dad together, they'll change their minds about us only having one pet." She nudged him with her elbow. "We're good as a team. Look what we did back at the cave!"

She took a deep breath. She and Cruise were better together, not fighting.

"I don't want you to stop challenging me

to competitions. I do want to stand out, but we're twins! We're always going to be close."

Cruise grinned. "Cool. Because I like hanging out with you. Plus, you're the only one who ever comes close to beating me."

Cali smirked. "You mean I'm the only one who beats you all the time?"

"We'll see about that."

Laughing, Cali said, "Come on, race you to the ceremony!"

Cruise sped off to the auditorium and Cali followed. They arrived at the very same time, laughing.

The principal and teachers were waiting onstage. Cali and the rest of the class took their seats while Cruise went up to join them.

"We are very excited to award the first-place medal in our first ever Royal Mermaid Rescue Crew School Tournament," Professor Korla said.

"Prince Cruise of Coquina, we are proud to name you Student of the Year." The principal put the medal around his neck.

Everyone cheered.

Cali was expecting her twin to zoom around the stage shouting *woo-hoo!* and pumping his fists in the air.

But he didn't. Instead, Cruise held the medal in his hands, staring at it. Then he said, "I can't accept this."

Chapter 11

Everyone in the crowd gasped.

"I don't understand," the principal said. "You worked so hard to win."

Cruise sighed. "I know. But Cali spotted the Night Star in the cave. So technically, she found it. And I didn't even pick it up. Bitey did!"

Principal Vanora laughed. "So Bitey should get the fifty points?" she asked.

"No, Cali should." Cruise handed the medal back to the principal.

Cali's stomach dropped. She couldn't believe it. Cruise won, but he was refusing the medal? She tried not to think about the bag of garbage.

The principal smiled at the crowd. "Well then, Cali, come up and get your medal!"

"Go on," Rio said, without the usual smile in her voice.

Cali swam to the auditorium stage. The principal put the medal around her neck. "I'm so proud of you! You worked so hard during the event. You collected so much glow coral—and litter! And you found the Night Star. We're so close to restoring the protective power of the magical Trident. Well done, Cali!"

Everyone cheered, but Cali's lip trembled. She thought winning this medal—and beating Cruise—would feel so good. She was finally standing out like she'd wanted to all along. But she felt horrible.

"What's wrong?" Professor Korla asked. "I expected you to be much more excited about this amazing honor."

Cali hung her head. "It's a wonderful honor. But I can't accept it." She took a deep breath. "When I was collecting litter, I met a mermaid taking out her trash. Some of it spilled, and I picked it up, but I didn't really collect it." She looked up at the principal through teary eyes. "I handed in the bag of trash anyway. I really only collected four, not five."

The auditorium was silent. But the bad feeling inside of her was going away.

"But you did find the Night Star," Cruise said. "Those fifty points put you ahead of everyone, even if you hadn't won the litter competition."

"But I didn't play fair. I don't deserve it." Cali took the medal off and handed it back to the principal.

"I didn't think I'd have such a hard time giving away this award," Principal Vanora said, chuckling. "But I'm proud of you both. It's hard to admit when you're wrong— when you've done something you don't feel right about."

"My insides felt very bad," Cali said.

"That's always a great guide. If it doesn't feel right, it probably isn't right," Professor Korla said. "It's a good lesson for us all."

The principal held up the medal. "Nixie, are you willing to accept this medal for Student of the Year?"

Nixie nodded and swam to the stage. She reached for Cruise and Cali's hands. "I'm so proud to be on the Rescue Crew with you two."

"I think we all learned a wonderful lesson here today," the principal said. "Thanks for being so honest." She held up the medal. "Nixie, you are the Student of the Year."

The crowd cheered while Cruise and Cali shared a big smile.

"Are you ready to swim home?" Cali asked.

"Yes," Cruise said. "Don't forget to bring the octopus so we can present our case to Mom and Dad—together."

Rio was waiting for Cali when she got off the stage. The octopus was bobbing beside her. "I'm so proud of you," Rio said.

Cali sighed. "I should have listened to you from the beginning. I knew it was wrong, but . . ."

"But you really wanted to win," Rio said. "Winning isn't everything."

"I know." She glanced at Cruise. "But I don't think this is the end of battling Cruise!"

"Of course not." Rio laughed. "You're still twins!"

Chapter 12

Cruise and Cali swam home with their seaponies and their pets. For once, they didn't race.

Cali crossed her fingers. "I hope Mom and Dad say yes!"

When they got to the castle, their parents were waiting outside. "So who won the tournament?" their dad asked. He looked back and forth between Cali and Cruise, waiting for an answer.

Cali laughed. "Neither of us!"

"Nixie won!" Cruise said.

Their mother raised an eyebrow. "You don't look very upset."

Cali shrugged. "We're not. We both did our best."

"That's all we ask for," their father said. "Doing your best doesn't mean you have to *be* the best."

That made Cali feel a lot better.

"But we have a question," Cruise said. Then he explained what happened with Bitey and the cave.

"Cruise loves Bitey, but I really like this sweet little octopus," Cali explained. "She'd love to live with us and she doesn't even have any ink! She won't be messy at all."

"And we're asking this together because we realized that we're better as a team than opponents," Cruise shared.

Their mother and father looked at each other and nodded. "I'm impressed," their mom said.

"This is exactly what we've been hoping to see from you two," their dad said.

"I think having your own pet is a great idea," their mom added.

"Awesome!" Cruise grinned.

"Thanks so much!" Cali said as the octopus twirled in a circle.

"What are you going to name yours?" Cruise asked Cali.

She thought for a moment. "You know, I think you were wrong when you said Bitey found the Night Star. The octopus found it and brought it there."

"I did! I found it in a cave," the octopus said through the Say Shell. "It's so sparkly!"

"So I'm going to name you Nighty! After the Night Star."

"I love it!" the octopus said.

Cali smiled at Cruise. "Thanks for helping me convince Mom and Dad."

Cruise hesitated for a moment. Then he hugged her.

Surprised, she hugged him back.

"Bet you I can hug you longer!" Cruise whispered.

"No way," Cali said, squeezing back and feeling lucky to have a twin brother. And thrilled that she'd finally realized they'd always be a team.

Welcome to the
ENCHANTED PONY ACADEMY,
where dreams sparkle and magic shines!

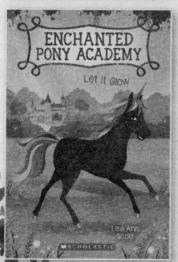

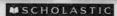

The Wish Fairy

One tiny fairy. Seven big wishes!

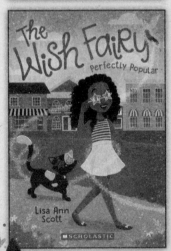

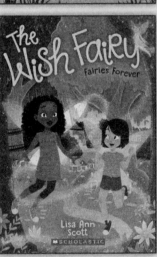

WISHFAIRY